My Psalms Through Seasons Of Life

How God has helped me lean on Him through all times in poems and what I call "psalms"

Written by Amber Wise

MY PSALMS THROUGH SEASONS OF LIFE

© 2024 by Amber Wise

Published by Fawcett

Paperback ISBN: 978-1-965683-28-6

All rights reserved. No part of this publication may be reproduced, stored in a retrieval system, or transmitted in any form or by any means – for example, electronic, photocopy, recording – without the prior written permission of the publisher. The only exception is brief quotations in printed reviews.

Photos are property of Amber Wise.

CONTENTS

Acknowledgements   1

1   Introduction   3

2   Laments: Mourning and Trust   6

3   Trust: Confidence and Security   36

4   Thanksgiving: Grateful and Joyful Worship   56

5   Wisdom: "Sermon Inspired"   77

6   Resurrection Series   102

7   Poems for friends; helpful to all   108

8   Reflective Poems   116

About the Author   141

ACKNOWLEDGMENTS

Thank you to my family and friends who helped me to see God in all areas of my life and inspired me to share with others.

Thank you to the many others who were praying and supporting this project- through many years in the making.

Most importantly, thank you to God, who has ultimately remained faithful and the one in control. I am so grateful that You are my father and I am your daughter. I am forever dependent on You.

1
Introduction

This book has been a long process and journey. While I am writing this, I still don't know if it's going to get published. My hope is that somehow these words, written down into "psalms," whether they get published or not, will be a testament to God. That people around the world will put their hope in Him, in a God that never fails. May Christians everywhere be united and grow in God no matter the season of life they are in.

These various "psalms," similar to the ones in the bible, fall under different categories. Some of the words you will read were written with great difficulty, even if they might have been easy to write, so to speak. Some were done in minutes, and some took days. It is a gift God has seemed to gift me with. It was hard to acknowledge I was not the one in control, more so that I could actually cry out to God as he wanted to know my mind. How crazy is that? God cared about me so deeply even though I struggled to understand and still do with some of the things I have had to go through. Yet, in each and every stage of life, there is purpose. God makes our life meaningful. I am so thankful that God has been able to bless me with this gift of writing where I could release the things that I was thinking to Him and allow it to be a place where I could communicate what I was facing in a more tangible way, even if I did not know the answers.

Honestly, I did not think I was going to publish these poems. Yet, over time, I started to share them with some close friends or people I knew. Some I had written to be shared but others only for my eyes and God's. As I began sharing them, both to encourage others and as an outlet for what I was going through, many commented on how it would be wonderful to get these written into a book. At first, I thought there was no way anyone would read them.

Although people did, and many were shared with others. People connected with the words through their own experiences or other people they knew.

Each and every one of us goes through many seasons in life, some occurring on the same day. No matter what season you are going through, whether you need encouragement, support, or a reminder to praise God... hopefully, one of these "psalms" will be just want you need to hear. May they encourage you to keep seeking Him.

2
Laments: Mourning and Trust

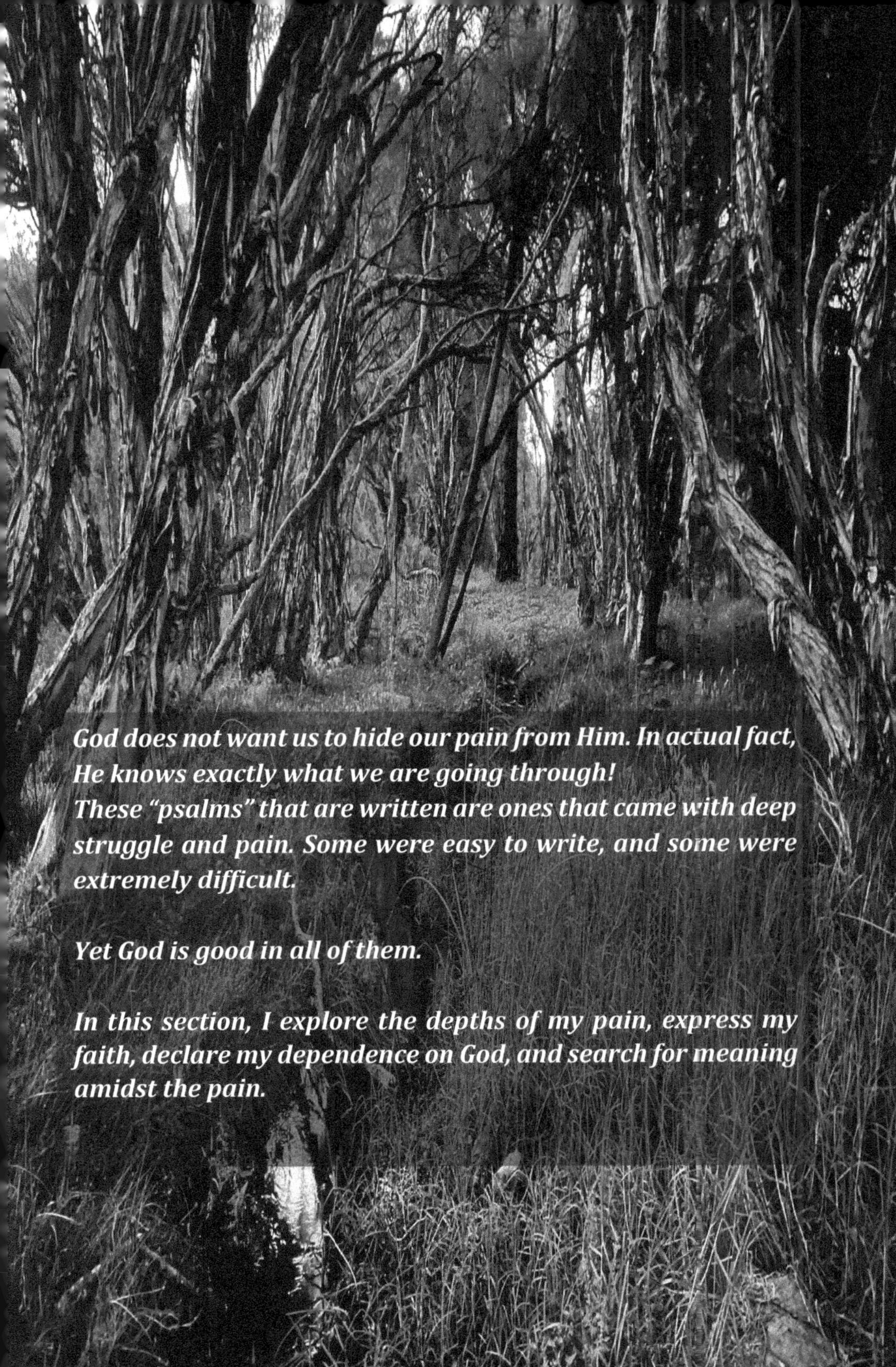

God does not want us to hide our pain from Him. In actual fact, He knows exactly what we are going through!

These "psalms" that are written are ones that came with deep struggle and pain. Some were easy to write, and some were extremely difficult.

Yet God is good in all of them.

In this section, I explore the depths of my pain, express my faith, declare my dependence on God, and search for meaning amidst the pain.

<u>True Rest:</u>

Lord, I do not understand what You are doing,
I do not understand what is happening.
Why all this pain, why here, why now?
But I trust You.
I look to You in the midst of the struggle,
Amidst this pain and sorrow.
Give me rest, I pray,
True rest in the situation that I face.
I know only this rest is found in You.
And while I may not be in comfort,
And long to escape from all this angst,
Please remind me of Your sovereignty.
You know what You are doing, Lord,
Even if I have no idea.
So, I'll rest in all that You do.
May You use this for Your glory,
May it not be for nothing.
Even if I grow just a little bit closer to You,
Just a little bit stronger in my journey with You,
It will all be worth it in the end.
I cannot wait for the day,
Where I can see You and hold You tight,
In Your loving arms.
How I long for that day where I'll be with You.

I've had enough of the pain.
Why don't You just take it all away?
I'm tired, and I'm angry,
Yet I'm beyond upset.
I've given up on what life has left.
I just want it to be over, my suffering gone.
Where is help coming from?
It's tiring to constantly say the pain I am in,
And in so much pain, I don't know where to begin.
What's worse is that I feel so self-centred.
I don't have the energy to be others-focused.
Maybe that's my problem, but how do I change,
When I'm screaming out in so much pain?
I want to help others; I really do,
Yet the energy I have is being constantly drained.
I don't know how I'm even going to get through.
Why am I hurting?
Why do I feel this way?
People say good will come from it,
Yet I don't know how that can be true.
How can this much suffering bring something that is good?
And even if it does, will it really be worth it?
Because at the moment, I don't know how.
Lord, deep inside, I know You have a greater plan.
I know victory is at Your hand.
But right now, I'm struggling; I really am.

<u>Million Mosaic pieces:</u>

A million pieces lying on the floor.
But really, what for?
Will the pieces ever be restored?
Will they one day be put back together to resemble an art piece, a mosaic?
But why did I have to be broken in the first place?
I know, I know, I turned my back away from You.
However, it wasn't until I was turning toward You that I felt I really started to break.
Surely, there could have been another way—one that does not require this much pain.
You say this is only for a little while; I just need to endure.
But, Lord, I'm not You, and so for me, it has seemed a really long time has already passed through.
One day, I may understand, but right now, I am struggling.
Please, Lord, keep my eyes focused and fixed on only You.
Surround me with Your presence to pull me through, so one day I'll be completely restored,
Where no more tears of pain will flow down my face,
but rather ones with only great joy.
So please, take my hand, Lord, and lead me there.

<u>Honesty in Suffering:</u>

I thought all was good.
I thought all was well.
I thought we'd finally figured it out.
Yet You seem to have other plans I am confused about.
However, before I go on, I just want to say:
Thank You for the little while where I felt fine,
When everything was great,
Where I felt like I could do things again,
And I could get through the things I needed to do.
Although now, to be honest, I'm struggling why.
Why could things not stay that way?
Why did the pain and sorrow have to come back?
So soon, I may add.
It's almost like You are teasing me.
Now, I don't know if this makes sense,
But it's as if it hurts more when it comes and goes.
I am not numb to the pain anymore,
And instead have to go through how it feels all over again.
The pain that I was accustomed to before,
Now feels new and hurts more than I thought.
While I know life isn't perfect,
I honestly thought I would at least get a little bit longer,
Where I could enjoy the time without struggling like this.
But You took all that away in what feels like a flash.
It's not like I had even turned away;
I was still praising Your name.
I thought I was still depending on You even in the joy I've just been
through.
Yet here, the pain and sorrow comes again.
Why can't it just go away for good this time?

I don't know Your plans.
I don't know Your thoughts.
I don't know why I am trusting You, Lord,
Because right now, I just want to scream:
Why are You doing this to me?
I don't understand.
Perhaps I never will.
But while I may never know why,
I do know this:
You have a plan in all of it.

<u>Pretending it's Fine (1):</u>

Everything inside of me wants to scream.
Why is this all happening?
The pain inside of me is so overbearing.
Can it please be silent for only a moment?
But when it is silent for a moment and then starts,
All I want to do is make it stop again.
Please don't keep going.
Why can't this be the end?
I feel the echoes of love try to surround me.
But all I feel sometimes is empty.
Can't anyone hear my desperate cry?
Please make this nightmare stop, please. Why?
People tell me that I'm brave, but really, I don't think that I am.
All I feel is wanting this pain to escape.
I don't feel brave; I just want this to vanish.
Sure, I may be enduring the pain, but not because I want to, but
rather I have to.
I am just being honest here; please believe me.
Sometimes something starts, and it is like, "Ooh, this feels bad,"
but quickly disappears.
Other times, it is like, "This is fine," and then rapidly ascends,
bringing about tears.
I feel like I just need to hold them in until I am in a place where I
can finally let them escape.
Why am I good at pretending it's fine when, really, it's not?
I think the answer lies with not wanting to worry anyone with my
struggles.
I am brave; I am strong… I can get through when really, I cannot.
But, Lord, You care.
Even through the ups and downs, it doesn't matter.

You care, Lord; You care.
You want me to pour out everything I have, not to hide it from
You, not to dismiss the pain I am feeling, but rather acknowledging
all of it.
Only then do You truly make me strong.
Even You wept, Lord... You care.
You care about me, the pain I am feeling, and You call me to draw
near to You.
Because even in the anguish and suffering, You care.
And, Lord, at the moment, that's all that's keeping me going.

<u>Pretending it's Fine (2):</u>

So I can tell people I'm fine when really I'm not.
I can tell people what they want to hear,
That everything's under control over here.
But all I would be doing is lying to them,
Even lying to myself deep inside.
As I try to suppress all the things I don't want to begin to describe,
I try to hide these things way down low,
Hoping they would go away on their own.
They will vanish someday if only I ignore them, right?
I can even tell You, Lord, that I am fine,
But You know me far better than that.
You know me better than I know myself,
Because those things I tried to hide—
Really, I was the one that was folly-trapped inside.
Those things were never going to go away on their own.
I thought things were meant to be easy,
That everything should be great.
But oh, how I was wrong.
You knew that all along.
You didn't want me or any of us to hide our weaknesses, failures,
struggles, or pain.
You not only held out Your arms to receive good,
But to receive all the baggage that we carry around,
Even the ones we try to hide down.
Yet, when we bring them to light,
You exchange them for us,
Holding us strong in Your presence, oh God.
Through leaning on You, we can see more of Your great good love.
You actually give that to us.
It may not be easy, but You do promise that,

One day, You will take all the struggles away.
Oh, how I can't wait for that day.
But even right now, we weren't designed to suppress.
We were not made to do this alone.
On this hard, good, down-and-up bumpy road,
So help us to be honest not only with You,
But with others, how we are doing too,
Letting the truth be told in our lives,
Of how You saved us despite what's going on deep inside.
Let us encourage each other and build each one up;
To lean on You through the good and rough.

<u>Out of Breath:</u>

Why this strange feeling?
I feel out of breath,
Desperate to get the oxygen in through these lungs of mine.
And while having to cough, it's hard to hide.
I am struggling to breathe inside.
But, Lord, may I draw closer near.
May I recognise my meek state.
I am not in control, no.
Rather, I am dependent on every breath that I take.
For example, the air that surrounds me—that was made by You.
You made my lungs and every single part of me.
More than that, everything that I see in sight is there because of
Your sovereignty.
So why am I surprised when things don't go the way I planned?
Why am I still afraid to ask for a helping hand?
I think it's okay when really it's not.
Why am I so stubborn, oh God?
I don't want to be a burden.
I don't want to be a hassle.
But really, why can't I see?
People love and care for me.
They want to help me when I am struggling.
They want me to be alright.
They want to help me not only in the good but the bad times.
So please help me to ask when I need and accept it when it is
offered to me.
But, Lord, more importantly, let me not just accept help from them
but ultimately You.
Lord, help me to see I am dependent on You—
Every step that I make, every breath that I take.

I wouldn't be here if it wasn't because of Your grace.
So, instead of taking for granted the life I live,
Please help me to remember the thanks that is due.
Help me to lean on You and all that You do.

Lord, I don't know anymore.
Or did I even know before?
Am I using this pain as an excuse,
Because I can still do the things I want to do?
Why do I struggle with some things,
When other things feel like a breeze?
I don't know why I am struggling.
Help me, please.
If I am using it as an excuse,
Please change my heart not to.
And if I am not,
Please hold me tight, knowing it's alright.
Whatever it may be, please help me see.
Please help me to cling to You, and please change me to be more
like You, my precious King.

<u>Rise:</u>

I will rise.
While right now, I don't feel that I can,
I will rise again.
I can be so sure.
Because Christ has risen before.
God never leaves His children behind,
And that is what He gladly calls me.
Even though sometimes I don't know why,
Through the ups and downs of valleys' core,
His love has always gone before,
Leading me through each and every part of life.
I no longer have to be in strife,
Because Christ will rise me up with Him,
Even out of any abyss, I swim.
Please, will you just listen?
Even though many answers remain hidden,
One day, we will stand face to face.
Oh my, I can't wait for that glorious day!
But even through this trench, I wander,
May He give me the patience to wait.
Because, for some reason,
This is the path I must take.

<u>Reality Not Feelings:</u>

Lord, where are You in the midst of this pain?
You say You are always here,
But yet, sometimes I don't feel You.
I am so glad Your reality is not based on my feelings though,
Because even through these deep depths where I wander,
You still find me.
Your love still surrounds me, even when it feels gone.
Help me to glance up toward You.
Help me forever to remain in Your word.
Help me to trust You.
Help me to seek You and know You more every single day of my
life.
Thank You, Father, for who You are.
Thank You that You are always there, no matter what.

<u>Give Me Strength:</u>

A million thoughts running through.
I can't get them out of my head.
I don't know what to think, what to do, what even to pray.
As I struggle with all these things in my brain,
Well, I assume they are, but maybe they are in my heart instead.
Wherever they are coming from, though,
I just know.
I am screaming at them to disappear,
Or at least come back one by one, not all at the same time now, do you
hear?
Maybe there's a reason they all just want to appear,
But why when I can't even concentrate on one…
I don't know what to do…
But I am looking to You.
You know all these things that I can't seem to grasp,
And while I can't seem to understand, I know You can.
Maybe that's the problem; I'm trying to keep them to myself.
I am trying to do this all on my own,
But Lord, if so, that changes right now.
While maybe You still won't take it all away,
I know deep inside that it will one day.
But until that day comes, this I do know:
With You by my side,
I will stay strong.
I will go on.

<u>Hidden No More:</u>

The pain and grief I feel inside,
I no longer want to hide.
But why, I'm not so sure,
Because, at the same time, I don't want anyone to know.

It's crazy, right?
While there probably needs to be a good balance of the two,
I know I just can't hide it anymore.

I'm probably afraid because I've hidden it for so long.

Where is this feeling coming from?
While yes, these things are painful,
In reality, keeping it down was making it hopeless.
I didn't notice this myself as I kept suppressing the pain,
Numbing myself while turning away.

But not dealing with the grief,
Just made it worse.

So now I need to bring it to light,
To undo all this hurt.

It's not just about bringing it out into the open,
But bringing it to You,
Putting it all on Your shoulders,
So I no longer have to carry it through.

Rather, I can let it release me,

No longer burdened with pain,
Because You carry it for me, including my shame.

Why was it shameful, I'm not sure,
Because pain is something we all have to endure.

Yet we don't have to do it on our own.

And so now I'm reaching out, both to You and to others You've
surrounded me with.

So, in all circumstances, rejoicing can be had.

Let us help each other stay strong in Your love,
Helping each other get through any obstacles we might face,
With You in control and ultimately leading the way.

Today was a whirl spin.
Pouring stop, pouring stop.
It reminds me of life and where I am at,
How quickly things can change in a flash.
One minute, everything's going well,
You think you have everything, or at least most things, under
control.
But then here comes the rain—
Whoosh, down it goes.
You no longer have control anymore.
But did you really have control before?
Although not many people like the rain,
We need it for things to grow.
I need it for growth.
I need it to remind me only God's in control.
No matter whether it's pouring down or whether the sun is
shining out,
Only God is in control.
These times are unpredictable, sure.
I don't know what will come next,
But I can trust that God does, and He uses these fluctuating
seasons for good—
Plans to prosper and not to harm,
Plans for a hope and a future.
And I know God's word is secure,
Secure in Christ, my Saviour.

Only You can rescue.
Only You can restore.
Only You can heal me and make me Yours.
Lord, I'm struggling to breathe;
It's like I'm drowning.
When I think I am swimming safely,
Another wave comes crashing around me.
It takes me down, down, down.
I need to resurface,
But yet I can't do it.
Only You can rescue.
Only You can restore.
Only You can bring me up from underneath this constant wave
feeling.

<u>Emptiness Peace:</u>

My mind is both so busy,
But then at the same time so empty.
It seems no thoughts are coming to mind,
As I just lay here quietly, listening to the echo of noise surrounding me outside.
I can hear the stillness of the night,
The crickets chirping, the air whispering so quietly.
I can feel my breath rising inside me, up and down, up and down.
But yet I can't fall asleep to this steady rhythmic beat,
Because inside my body is screaming,
"Please don't make me."
I'm confused; I know I need sleep to recharge,
But yet, it's a struggle for me to sleep through the night.
The pain is either intense or just there, niggling at me, forcing me to stay awake.
And when I do get good sleep,
It seems I am more tired the next day.
How is this possible?
I wish I knew why this was the case.
Yet despite this, I have peace—
Peace that it won't always be this way,
Peace that one day there will be no more pain,
Peace that not only will I get more sleep but that the whole world will be restored,
Back to how it should be,
With praises and glory given to God—the true King.

Lord, let me leave this situation in the past.
What's done is done.
I need to move on.
Calm my overwhelming thoughts.
May I take what I need moving forward,
And leave the things behind in which I have no control over,
But take the elements I need to know so I can grow.
Be with the others in this situation.
Please help them to do the same.
Help us to love each other as You've shown us,
With Your mercy and Your grace.
Each and every one of us makes mistakes,
And has our own battles that we face.
So may we be humble, compassionate, and gentle,
Even when we feel we are about to break.
We do not know the other person's struggle,
Or the pain they may carry inside.
So, let's move forward with kindness in our eyes.
Lord, You know each and every one of us,
Beyond what the world can see.
So, remind us of the bigger picture,
Not just the viewpoint we see underneath.
Rather, give us peace from up above,
And work through us to demonstrate Your love.

<u>Burden Bearer:</u>

Pain, loss, grief—
Emotional roller coaster.
Crying for relief,
Not knowing why,
Not feeling well,
Desperate for help.
Not wanting to be a burden,
Not wanting to pull anyone down into your spiral.
Just trying to get through life's battle.
But then somebody comes along,
Bringing a shoulder to cry on,
Bringing a listening ear.

Not judgmental, but wanting to see you win.
Wanting you to overcome the struggle.
Helping you face what you are going through,
Offering advice and words of encouragement,
Lifting the burdens right off you.

Tears of thankfulness flow down your face,
As you don't know what words to say.

If that was you, you would be over the moon,
Thankful that someone came to your rescue.

Even when you didn't know what to do,
Wouldn't that be wonderful if that person was you?
We can be a burden bearer,
We can bring joy to someone's day.

Even when it may cost us a lot,
We can help others to overcome,
As together we can be strong.

But more importantly,
We can show them the life that Christ has for us.

As without Him, well, the world is pointless.

My mind?
My heart?
What is it?
Why are these thoughts bubbling up inside of me?
A feeling I cannot name—
It's peculiar, odd, strange.
Why is it stirring deep within?
Why can I not put a name to it?
I don't know what is going on,
But I know it needs to go.
Somehow, I must shake it off.

<u>Hard to Sleep:</u>

I lay down on the bed—
Something I have come to dread.
Perhaps tonight won't be too bad;
Maybe I will actually be glad.
Tonight might be the night I easily fall asleep.
All I need to do is take a leap.
So I lie down on the bed.
At first, I thought it was just in my head,
But then the burning started to grow,
Creeping up through the body super slow,
Making the pain feel more intense.
Why is this happening again?
Deep breath, ignore, I tell myself,
Trying to let the pain heal itself.
Deep breath, deep breath—Lord, save me.
Eventually, I drift off to sleep.

<u>Pressures of Work:</u>

Lord, sometimes I come home mentally and exhaustingly drained.
Work has sent me through the emotions.
I am not sure if I can do that again,
But, Lord, You know each battle that I face.
Help me to switch this brain off and pray.
You are the one in control.
You are the one that holds all things.
I cannot keep focusing on the endless tasks overwhelming me,
Or the pressures that this job brings.
Instead, I need to surrender it to Thee.
Lord, take this cup of burden off me,
And help me get some sleep.
I am not in control.
I can only take it to You.
And so, let me surrender it all at Your feet.

Our students are made in the image of God,
Whether they know this or not,
Or whether they understand Christ,
They are still made in God's image.
And so, they deserve our utmost care and respect,
Even if at times it may be hard to give.
We need to be careful about this.
The best thing to do when it is hard is just to stop and pray to God.
Lord, You care about this child in front of me.
Right now, I am struggling.
I want to show them Your loving care.
Please set aside my thoughts and provide me with Yours.
What would You do in this situation, Lord?
I pray that You would help me right now,
So I can lovingly care for them now.
Hopefully, through us, they might be able to see,
The wonderful beauty of our loving King.

3
Trust: Confidence and Security

These psalms are written relating to trust in God. The words written offer confidence and security in God and Him only. Some are a celebration of the hope we have in God, while others are a reminder to keep trusting Him, even in difficult times.

In this section, I explore the agape love, wavering but unyielding faith and trust in God.

<u>True Purpose:</u>

All through my life, I've had trouble and pain.
I'm thrown down by all that life pelts at me,
But maybe this is for a greater gain,
A better purpose that I cannot see.

There's a superior power that I can feel,
Something that's drawing me ever so still;
It's so strong it just makes me want to kneel,
Holding such splendour and marvellous will.

Holding me so close, I can hardly breathe.
I don't want Him to ever let me go.
In wonder and awe, I'm in disbelief;
I'm nearly ready to just overflow.

How can He love me so sincere and true?
A sinful daughter, I just wish I knew.

I'm worried, stressed, and anxious.
Put your hope in God.
I'm weary, tired, and worn.
Put your hope in God.
I'm hurting, in pain, and discomfort.
Put your hope in God.
I'm confused, I'm lost, I don't understand.
Put your hope in God.
He will deliver you.
You are not alone.
God will lead and bring you through.
Put your hope in God.
He will be with you.

Lord, only You offer comfort,
Hope that will never disappear.
So, when we are in a state of despair,
May we draw closer near.
However, may it not just be when we are struggling,
May it not just be when we are in dismay,
But through every situation that we face,
May You cover us with Your grace.
May we not think we have it all under control,
Because ultimately, we don't.
We are dependent on You, Lord, for every single thing this life will bring.
May we willingly cling to Thee.

Lord, may I not forget You in the midst of this sorrow and pain.
May I not forget You whether the sun shines or fades away.
May I always remember how good You are,
And may I hold on to the fact You always care.
Because even though sometimes I may feel neglected,
Although my reflections may be warped,
You are always good towards Your children,
In which You gladly call me Yours.
I am Your child, dearly loved.
I am not forsaken nor forgotten.
I was never abandoned,
Because You never left my side.
You never turned Your back away,
Even when all hope seemed lost.
You are the giver of all good gifts,
And Your presence is the greatest present I could ever receive.
Lord, I am Your child,
And You dearly love me.

<u>Goodness of God:</u>

Lord, You indeed give what is good because You are good.
You are right beside me even when I do not feel You.
You never leave me nor abandon me.
You were right there the entire time, holding me tight.
May I cling to the truth,
That You are turning my battle into victory,
You are getting me to that finish line,
You are not against me, even when it feels like I may be drowning.
If anyone can get me through,
It will only be the one who wins every battle,
Who wins every time,
And that one is only You.

<u>The Lord is Near:</u>

The Lord is near.
The Lord is near, right beside me,
Holding me tight in His loving arms.
Therefore, I do not need to be anxious.
I do not need to be afraid.
I am not going to drown, even when I feel like I am drowning.
I am not going to fall hitting rock bottom,
Even when I feel I am falling with no one to catch me.
May I remember the Lord is near.
You, Lord, will break my fall.
You will catch me.
You are near.
My worries, my fears, my troubles, my strife,
Are nothing before You.
May I surrender all.
May I fall from the trap of the lies that You left me,
And may I fall into Your arms, remembering Your promise,
That You are near.
Thank You that You hold me tight and dearly love me
unconditionally.

<u>Blessing in Suffering:</u>

Suffering can be a blessing,
If you take the right amount of time to grieve.
If you do not quickly jump over it,
Like a boat zipping across the sea.
If only able to be opened wide,
You may be able to see the beautiful treasure inside.
I'm not saying this is painless or easy to endure,
But through wrestling with the pain,
You may be surprised to see.
A mysterious peace surfacing to the shore.
A blessing indeed just for you and me in our moments of grief.
God wants all of you, even the bits we want to submerge.
He invites us to pour out everything we have to Him,
Even those moments we think are not worth a single thing.
Our weaknesses, our failures, our struggles, and our pain.
God cares even about these we often want to hide away.
But the fact is, deep treasures can be brought about even in times
of suffering.
So pour out your hearts to God, just hold on and see the comfort
this will bring.

<u>Vulnerability:</u>

When we are vulnerable,
When we don't hold back,
Instead, we are giving everything, every corner and crack.
Through these cracks, something marvellous begins to unfold.
We are no longer trapped;
We are free from our ensnaring thoughts.
When we let down our guard,
We let others in,
But more than that,
We draw even closer,
To our redeeming King.

Where to begin, oh where to start?
I thought by now You would depart.
But oh, how foolish I was, You not only stayed,
But You worked wonders and changed my heart to this day.
Although I was drifting far away,
You remained close and marked the way.
I wouldn't be where I am today,
If it wasn't because of Your mercy and grace.
You made me who I am,
And a child of Yours, I will always remain.

<u>Loved by a King:</u>

I am loved.
I am loved by a King.
I am loved even beyond what I can see.
How could God love someone like me?
He's everlasting, glorious beyond measure, and faithful,
Yet full of mercy and grace.
He takes my guilt and shame away.
He's majestic, powerful, holy, and worthy of all praise,
Yet He calls me by name.
He's abundantly good, gracious, and just,
Yet He calls me His child.
He's compassionate, slow to anger, and rich in love.
I don't deserve this love by God,
Yet He reaches down,
And pulls me tight in His arms.
And since it's only because He chooses to give,
I am now eternally His.
I am forgiven, I am dearly loved, I was called by name, and now I
stand a child of God today.
Yet now, this can never be taken away.

<u>All in Your Hand:</u>

Though sometimes I don't understand,
Quite often, in fact,
I have to pause and remind myself that it's all in Your hands.
Because it's You who will act.
You are the one that holds all the pieces.
I only hold a few.
I don't need to know all the reasons,
Because You hold the true view.
You know all that is going on.
I just need to trust in You,
As You have it all under control.
Even if I don't know the ins and outs,
It's You who is directing it now.
So let me be reminded of You and Your goodness,
Reminded that while I only see my part,
You see and hold the whole big picture, God.

<u>The Father's Love:</u>

The Father cares for each of His children.
He's desperate to find them,
To bring them back home.
He wants to love, care, and protect them,
Making sure they stay out of harm's way.
Caring for their every need,
Making sure they are secure in Him.
He will never forsake or abandon them.
He will never leave them alone.
He loves and cares for them
More than they will ever know.
So give your life to the Father.
He will never leave your side.
He loves it when we come back home.
He rejoices at the sight.

<u>God is in Control:</u>

Lord, You have a plan;
You work everything out for Your good.
I may not know what You have in store,
But You knew before the world began,
Where I would be, Oh Lord.
Isn't that amazing?
One that I have often explored.
Your word is unfailing;
It is something that cannot be shaken.
Even though the world changes,
I know that through the ages,
I will not be forsaken.
Even though I may not understand,
Although my thoughts may be misleading,
You hold everything in Your hand.
You are the one preceding.

Lord, help me to stop and think;
Breathe, pause, just listen.
Listen to Your voice and what You have to say.
Not get caught by my mind swirling away,
Not thinking about things that I have still to do,
But rather to be reflective and trusting in You.
I don't have to worry;
I don't have to stress.
I can give it to Your hand,
So I can stop, pause, and listen to Your voice.
I can breathe, focus, and pray,
Knowing that only You are in control.
No matter what things are on my plate,
I can trust You;
I can seek You;
I can just be in Your presence.
I can give all that I am to You,
And marvel at Your goodness.

<u>Faith even in Suffering:</u>

Faith wouldn't be real faith if you only believe when things are
good.
Terrible things happen; who are we to know why?
Believe in God and His goodness,
Or believe the world is pointless and random.
Whatever makes you happier, you might say,
But God's not indifferent to our pain.
The world is full of brokenness and hurt,
Yet that doesn't mean it was because of Christ.
Sometimes something happens, and we don't get to know why,
At least not in this earth time.
However, even in the depths of despair,
We can trust in the goodness of God.
True faith is trusting God is always good,
No matter what life may bring.

<u>Be like a Child; Dependent on God:</u>

I wonder if you have ever thought,
About how a child is readily taught.
How they are, on the 'whole', meek and mild;
They are dependent on their parent's hand.
You see, what I am most talking about is a child's willingness to be
led.
The parent is the one who provides for their needs.
At least, in a perfect relationship, the parent leads,
And the child humbly accepts and trusts their parent will provide
for them.
Wouldn't it be cool if we were just like that with God?
Where we willingly trust in Him above,
Even though to us it may seem odd?
We were taught to fully love;
We were designed to be fully blessed.
God is the one who blesses us;
He wants to be the one who gives us good gifts.
If, like a child, we are willingly led,
As He deeply knows and cares about us,
Let's be like a child, dependent on God.

<u>Frailty of life:</u>

It surprises me sometimes to think,
How much we plan our life to be;
Yet our life can disappear in a flash.
Our hopes and plans can quickly dash.
We do not control life,
As much as we think we can.
Our life is only dependent on Your hand.
Only You are in control;
Only You hold the future plan.
Our life is only frail;
It can disappear in such a short moment of time,
Gone in a blink of an eye.
But, Lord, You know—
You know before the beginning of time.
You crafted us, Your perfect design.
May we remember we are not in control;
Instead, may we give everything to You,
Knowing that we do not have to fear,
Knowing that while our life is only frail,
You still care and love us so.
Therefore, we don't have to be afraid, whatever this life may hold,
As we can cling strongly to Thee,
No matter what the future brings.

4
Thanksgiving: Grateful and Joyful Worship

These psalms are one of praise and thanksgiving to the Lord who created us and is above all things. May these encourage you to keep praising YAHWEH! (Lord of all)

In this section, I explore the themes of gratitude, praise for the provision of God and also express the joy brought by Him.

<u>Thankfulness:</u>

'Thanks' is something you can do,
Every day of your life,
No matter the situation,
No matter your strife.

There are so many things to be thankful for—
So many things that we often ignore.
Just the fact that we are alive, breathing right now,
Is its own miracle we should talk about.
But there are other things too, like the clothes on our back,
Or the fact that we don't have to scavenge around,
For food that we just put in our mouths.

Maybe you can walk and talk;
I think that's something you ought to be thankful for.
Or maybe you can't, that's okay.
You can show others how you do things every day.
Through you, they may see the great, wonderful treasure,
Of giving thanks no matter the weather—
No matter how you are feeling,
No matter what you are going through,
There's always something to be thankful for.
But who should our thanks be to?
No, it's not the person sitting next to you,
But rather the Maker of all creation,
The one who gives us eternal life if only we believe in Christ.

The good thing about thankfulness,
Is it's not about us;
Rather, it's about Jesus and what He's done.

You see, we were once destined for death,
But He took on our evil, our rejection of God,
And paid the price we ought to pay for.
He rose us up again with Him,
So now, our relationship with God,
Can once again be restored.
So, really, no matter the situation you are going through,
You can always thank God for this marvellous gift—
That you once were dead, but now you are alive in Him.

<u>Beyond Thankful:</u>

We have so many things to be thankful for.
Here's a few things to remind us when we are a bit unsure.

Just the fact that we are alive, breathing right now,
Is its own miracle we should talk about.
But there are other things too, like not having to scavenge around,
For food that we just put in our mouths.

Then there's the great company of our pets—
Whether that's cats or dogs, or having spiders with family's
support.

We are thankful that, at the moment, we are not in lockdown,
And that we can freely wander around.
We are thankful for our beds.
As someone said, "I'm thankful for my mustard yellow bedspread."
It's great we have blankets and clothes to keep us warm,
Especially when we feel a little bit cold.

We are thankful for our weekends, a time to relax.
While some like the fact that there's nothing to do,
Others like sport or a card game or two.
We are definitely thankful for friends, family, youth group, and
church,
Because even in challenges, we can be sure,
We will always be surrounded by encouragement, love, and
support.
Hopefully, ultimately, through it all,
We will be reminded that God is always with us,
No matter, even if times get a little bit tough.

So let's remember always, no matter where life goes,
That we can always thank God for the blessing He bestows—
This marvellous gift, freely given to us,
Making us alive through what Jesus did on that cross.

Made in collaboration with our youth group
(August, 2020)

Who alone deserves the praises,
Is it me, or is it you?
No, rather, it belongs to God,
Now and forevermore, it's true.
He's the Maker of all creation,
The one who gives us life,
Both right here on earth and also yet again in Christ.
He saved us from the pits,
The deep destruction we were in.
We should be facing gloom,
But instead, we are facing Him.
He's the one who is holy, good, and just,
While we were, let's face it, muck.
Yet He took on our unrighteousness and made us right in Him.
So, who deserves the praises?
Well, really, only Him.

Although we are all uniquely different,
Each having our own gifts,
We were made to work together,
To praise the Lord God forever.
He is our creator,
He destined us to be.
Without Him, we would not be here,
No matter your beliefs.
However, I hope that you can trust me,
Even more, that you can see,
Our entire thanks belong to God,
Through all eternity.

Thank You, God,
For making me, me.
I cannot disregard,
Who You created me to be,
A child of Yours,
So wonderfully made.
I want to ensure,
I am praising Your name,
Because You deserve the praise, Lord.
You created me,
So I just want to thank You,
For making me, me.

<u>The Greatness of God:</u>

(Inspired by Psalm 71)
I love the Lord.
Despite the hopeless situation I was in, the deep sorrow and pain,
Ultimately, spiritually dead with nowhere to go,
I cried out to God, and He answered me.
More than that, He brought me from death to life.
How worthy is God?! How great He is!
He is full of compassion, mercy, and love.
He is righteous, holy, and just.
Graciously, He brought me to Him, bringing me from death to life
in His name.
Therefore, I will continuously praise God forever.
I will serve and live for Him for what He has done in my life,
Thanking God for all He is.
Praise the Lord!

Boast in nothing but the cross of Christ.
Without Him, we have nothing at all.
While I am a sinner, Jesus is my Saviour.
My only hope is what He has done for me.
Jesus crucified is my only boast.

<u>Boast Only in Christ:</u>

What little I have, what little I give,
Is nothing compared to Him.
I have lots to boast in, but nothing is mine.
Rather, I only have all because of Christ.
He's the one that deserves all praise.
He's the one that saved me from the grave.
He's the one who gives me peace.
He's the one that brought me to my knees.
He's the one who gave His life to save mine.
Because He's the one who conquered death,
He's the one that rose up to life again.
He's the one that sets us all free,
If only we believe in Him.
He restores us, redeems us, loves us more than we know.
So, really, what have I to boast in?
Nothing of mine.
Rather, it's only my Saviour, Jesus Christ.

<u>Rejoice:</u>

How crazy but awesome is it,
That we can rejoice and thank God in all circumstances,
Every single one.
Whether crazy, uncertain, painful, or hard,
Whether wonderful, amazing, full of great joy,
We can be thankful and rejoice to our Lord.
Nothing can separate us from His love.
We have a beautiful, gracious, and loving Saviour who will always
be with us.
So even in the hardest times, we can rejoice,
Because even though life can be incredibly hard,
What amazing and sure hope we have in Christ!
We can thank God for His good control,
No matter what life may bring.
We can thank God for His good, pleasing, and perfect will.
He will always sustain us even when things feel doomed.
How scary it would be if God was unloving and deceiving,
But the great thing is He's not.
He's far more honourable and worthy of praise.
He's our great Saviour God.

<u>Glorious God:</u>

God is far more glorious, holy, and majestic than we could imagine.
Yet He's not our servant or taskmaster-driven.
Rather, He's the King, our Saviour, light of the earth.
He's holy, incredible, and full of all worth.
So may we praise and glorify His name all day,
Not because we have to but because we want to praise His name.

<u>Names of God:</u>

God,
Where to begin?
I'm just in awe of Your holiness.
You have so many names to describe Yourself,
But even then, that doesn't even begin to capture Your majestic
self:
King of kings, Prince of Peace, Lord of lords,
Wonderful Counsellor, God Most High,
Peace of peace, Revealer of mysteries.
You are unchanging, patient, and full of all compassion.
You are our Deliverer, Defender, and gracious to us,
Maker of all things, immortal, Helper of the fatherless,
Holy, just, faithful, and true.
You are the fountain of life, almighty, the author and perfector of
our faith.
You are the God of all comfort, the God of all kingdoms of the
earth.
More than that, the God of heaven and earth, who does wonders,
who sees, who is merciful throughout all of history.
You are head of the body, the church, over every power and
authority.
You are full of love, You are magnificent, You are generous, You
are kind.
You are the reason for our hope, refuge from the storm.
You are our shelter, our Saviour, Shepherd, and Overseer of our
souls.
You are wonderful, worthy, unchanging Yahweh.
You say You are I AM,
Which encompasses more than these few names combined.
There are so many more, and yet, although we don't deserve it,

You say You are our Father and call us Your child.
So, although it's not much, all I can really say is:
Thank You, Father, for who You are,
More than I will be able to understand or describe.
Praise be to You, my God.

<u>Blessed in Support:</u>

Thank You, Lord, for all the support.
It has been a blessing to see,
How You were providing for me.
Even though inwardly I was screaming,
You were calming my anxieties.
You've provided me with amazing people,
Who have shown me Your love,
Who have helped kept me strong.
Without them and without You, who knows where I would be?
But thanks be to You, God, I'm still standing.
You love me more than I could ever dream.

Lord, it's amazing You provide,
Even despite uncertainties I have.
You put that all aside,
Because it's what You have planned.
You know every little detail,
Every piece of the puzzle.
You know the plan from day one;
It's all in Your majestic hand from the start.

<u>True Joy:</u>

Joy isn't just when times are going well.
Joy can be found in every season of life.
How can that be so,
When isn't the definition of joy about happiness and success?
Well, yes,
But something deep has changed,
Which enables people to have joy,
Not only through laughter and smiles,
But when our hearts may be breaking inside.
Joy can be found in every season of life,
Because true joy is only found in Christ.

Uniquely Different; Wonderfully Made:

We are all uniquely different, which is a great thing to be.
Each and every one of us, sophisticatedly made,
In the image of God is what we became.
Although sometimes we think different,
We were all created with different gifts and personalities, you
could say,
So that through our differences we can achieve something greater,
Giving God the thanks and glory throughout all the ages.
Because You deserve the praise, Lord.
You are the one who created us.
So may we give You the thanks and glory through all eternity,
As it is through You we are wonderfully made.
And so, Lord, we want to thank You today.

5

Wisdom: "Sermon Inspired"

I have written these psalms either based on sermons or my own bible reading. These words are an expression of what I have heard and what God has placed in my heart.

In this section, I share the wisdom about faith in Christ's grace, sacrifice, and resurrection

Saved by Grace:

By God's grace, I'm saved.
Lovingly, He brought me up from the grave.
This may seem like a strange thing to say,
But in reality, I was nothing without Him.
I was spiritually dead; even worse, I deserved to be punished,
For rejecting God, my Creator, the One who had made me.
Instead of thanking Him,
Shamelessly, I spat in His face,
Wanting to rule myself my way.
But what did He do?
He forgave me.
Instead of being holy and just,
He took that punishment I rightly deserved,
That rightful anger, and laid it all on Jesus, my Saviour.
Through Him, I have a new life.
The debt I once had is no longer mine;
Christ took it all for me,
And instead, I got His glory.
Because of Him, I am holy,
To stand before God, being restored.
Not because of what I had done but because of what Christ has
done for me.
So thank You, Jesus, for this wonderful gift,
That now I can stand before God righteous and holy.
You deserve the praises and glory.
So thank You for all You have done for me,
Taking my hopeless state and turning it into great rejoicing.
Thank You, Jesus, for resurrecting me.
Thank You for giving me new life for all eternity.

<u>Full in Christ:</u>

All our fullness is found in Christ;
Nothing else can truly satisfy.
Although we often turn to this or that,
We can be sure that it's a lost cause,
Because, in the end, it leaves us discontent,
Crying out for more,
Wondering where next to go,
Where next that will satisfy our empty souls.
However, instead of looking any further,
We should be looking to Christ our Saviour,
Without adding a single thing.
Because although some may disagree,
Christ is all we will ever need.

Who makes us powerful when we feel unable,
Or humbles us when we feel indestructible?
Without God, we are weak.
Our efforts do not stand;
They are not eternal.
But our God and Saviour Jesus is for sure.
He gives us strength when times are tough;
He reminds us who we are.
Without Him, we are merely feeble;
We do not stand the test.
How could we even try?
But with God, we are able,
To succeed beyond our expectations.
Because our God is so great,
He conquers everything.
So let's praise His name,
Because without Him, we could do nothing,
Nothing of value at all.
So thank God next time He works through you.
It's a wonderful gift, a blessing indeed.
God makes us strong when we are only weak.

<u>Fallen:</u>

So we think we are good or at least okay,
But how many times do we turn from our God every day?
We lie, we cheat, we steal;
We follow other things instead of following Him.
We put others down and our needs number one.
We are selfish, we are prideful, we are all of the above.
Whether or not you are following God, you are following something,
Whether that be sports, celebrities, popularity, or money.
These are just a few things it could be.
But consider this: who are you following or pursuing?
Because maybe having a relationship is the top of your priority,
And this is not a relationship with God but with somebody else,
Which isn't necessarily wrong, but the fact that you are searching for them above God yourself.
God created you; He made you to be.
But instead, you have rejected Him throughout your history.
Yes, that's right, we were fallen at birth.
Now, only Jesus can save and set us free.
But remember the cost that this would bring;
He laid down His life for you and me.

<u>True Sin:</u>

Lord, remind me I'm not perfect;
Please remind me of my sin,
That I need You to save me,
From the guilt within.
Help me not to see it and think that all is fine,
Because I have rejected You, the One who is holy and divine.
Instead of following You, I chose to follow anything else.
Instead of following Your majestic self,
I chose to put my wants first.
Instead of my own needs,
Because I actually need You, Lord, more than anything.
My sin brings upon disaster,
Punishment well deserved.
Help me please realise how serious sin can be,
Since through sin, I reject You as my King.
However, because of Your mercy and grace,
You took the punishment from me.
And not only that, You restored me,
Making me once again holy.
It ended up costing me nothing,
While it cost You dearly.
You did not turn Your face;
Rather, You looked sin in the eye.
You took it off me,
And now I cannot deny,
How much it cost You for setting me free.
So help me, Lord Jesus, to see the severity of my sin.
Change, shape, and mould me to be more like You,
My precious King.

<u>Worship:</u>

Worship,
What will it do? What will it bring?
In my heart, I know what is true.
Worship brings me closer to You.
It reminds me of my failures while reminding me of the hope I
have received,
The saving wonders of my salvation You gave to me.
And You are making sure I remain steadfast in Your word.
Since without worship, I'll be conditioned by the world's culture;
I will be distorted by my prejudice.
I will not be reminded of the guilt I have within,
And I will not remember the cost You bore so that I could be set
free.
In true worship, You touch not only my head but my heart.
My attention is centred on the personal and decisive words of You,
God.
It enables me to see how much I need You as my King.
I am at peace and secure in You, no matter what the world brings.

<u>Free in Christ Alone:</u>

Lord, we are blessed through You and You only.
You keep us safe in You; You hold us fast.
Your love is amazing, never changing.
Keep us, mould us, shape us.
Make us more who You created us to be.
Focus our attention and mind on Christ,
Not on earthly pleasures that so often limits, so often bounds, and
enslaves us,
Engulfs us in this downward spiral of danger we can't escape from.
We are only free in You.
We are only truly free and have everlasting peace in You, O Lord.
Please help us to see,
Help us to experience Your incredible, mind-blowing, free-setting
love,
That only You can give.
The very piece of the puzzle that makes us really, truly, and
everlastingly complete is You.
Again, please help us see and cling to You earnestly, despite the
worldly pressures, desires, and passions that often takes us so far
away.
Keep Your promise, we pray.

<u>Restored in Christ:</u>

My precious Lord Jesus,
Is no longer dead.
Although once held, He conquered death.
He took on my guilt and shame,
The punishment I should have paid,
And He rose up from the grave.
Because of this, I stand free;
No more shame or guilt hanging off me.
I don't deserve to be set free,
But because of Christ's sacrifice,
My debt has been cleaned,
Not just past but present and future as well.
And because of this, I can see,
My precious Lord Jesus standing before me saying:
"My dear child, come.
My sacrifice is more than enough.
You no longer have to hide.
More than that, you can stand holy.
You can be with me in future glory.
But even right now on this earth,
I am still there with you,
Cheering you on with this race I set for you.
Although darkness is still present,
Know that my judgment is being withheld,
So more people can stand with you and Me on that final day,
Where full, just judgment will reign.
But for those who trust in My sacrifice,
That day will be the happiest of their lives.
Don't you see, I want people to be with Me,
But a choice has to be made,

To either accept or reject this gift I display.
Anyone can turn and be saved,
No matter what they've done.
My sacrifice was more than enough;
The sting of death has been cut off.
So what are you waiting for, child?
Go tell this glorious, great news of mine,
That absolutely anyone can turn and be healed,
That this life can no longer define you,
Unless that's what you choose."

<u>Come Home to the Lord:</u>

Come home,
Come home to the Lord.
He's waiting for you with arms open wide.
He's waiting to hold you and hug you tight.
Through His death and resurrection, no more guilt or shame hangs
over our heads,
Because we are completely forgiven by the blood, He shed.
He rose up from the grave and gave us new life,
And so the chains that once held us can no longer confine.
We can run towards Him because, by Him, we are free.
It is a wonderful mystery how this can be,
How He can continue to love us even when we constantly shut
Him out.
But even so, He still cries out,
"Come home, child,
Come home to Me,
Come home."

I don't know how, and I don't know why,
But all I know is God is holding me tight.
Sometimes, I just want to cry and disappear.
Why am I here?
Other times, I feel like a royal;
Nothing can ever get past me, your majesty.
But no matter what it is,
Something inside is strangely missing,
And the more I grasp this thread,
The more I pull and tug,
I realise I'm missing God.
Well, at least I am.
God, on the other hand, never left my side.
Instead, He was keeping me close.
He was the one who opened my eyes to see,
That I really needed Him, not just for a little while but all eternity.
I am not God because there's only one,
And that's Him, not me.
So this means I need to stop with the lies that I know it all or that I
am not worth it at all,
Because God changes my identity;
He restores it for His glory.
I don't know how, and I don't know why,
Except that He's the one changing me, holding me tight,
Never letting me go,
Not later on, and certainly not tonight.
I am surrounded and held by His love that burns bright.

<u>Come Home:</u>

Come home,
Come home, My child.
I will forgive you no matter what you've done.
You are loved deeply;
You are precious in My sight.
While you may be in remorse and want to escape,
While you are running away, just to hide from your disgrace,
I am running towards you with My arms open wide.
Secure yourself in Me, My child.

<u>True Freedom:</u>

Free to love,
Free to surrender all,
Free not to live for ourselves, you know,
Because that will only bring destruction.
Who would want that when we can bring joy?
We can bring life to others around,
A peace that can never be broken down.
Free to serve,
Free to give,
Free to make our lives His,
Free for Christ to live in us,
And to do the work of God.

<u>True Saviour:</u>

If I was there when Jesus rose again,
I, too, would not have believed my eyes,
As three days earlier,
I witnessed this man die.
Yet now, standing right in front of me,
I can see that He's alive.
What does this mean now?
Surely, this man is more divine.
This man, this person I now behold,
Can only truly be the Saviour who came to save the world.
And while today we cannot see Him,
I still believe it's true,
That Jesus died and rose again to save both me and you.
While I believe He is my Lord and Saviour, who is He for you?
Will you believe He is your Lord and Saviour, too?

<u>True Living Hope:</u>

We have hope,
A living hope.
It cannot be quenched by fire;
It does not burn out when trouble arrives.
It will always survive.
Why? Because of Christ.
It is living because He rose again.
It is living because He defeated death.
It cannot be taken from us.
It's a guaranteed, unshakeable hope,
Because it comes from our Saviour, Lord.
We know Jesus is in heaven preparing His place,
For us one day to reign,
If we hope in His name.

<u>Generosity:</u>

How generous is the Father?
The generosity that He gives,
It is far beyond measure,
Far greater than we think.
While our generosity,
Is often for selfish gain,

This is not even close to what God did and continues to do.
Just take, for instance, what happened on the cross,
Where Jesus took our place.
What did Jesus have to gain?
We are all quick to say us,
But really, come on.
Like sure that may be correct,

But why when we are the ones who put Him there?
If not you, well, I know it was certainly me,
Since I, too, rejected my King.
I wanted to be in control of my life,
And so Jesus had to die.
Did He really have to?
Well, in some sense, yes,

In order to save the people who put Him there.
It's a little bit roundabout, I know,
But is the generosity shown being made a little more clear?
I am still not a perfect angel over here,
But thankfully, I don't have to be.

Through the generosity, my Heavenly Father showed to me,
I am saved, I am free, no more debt to pay.

Yet I was not the one to have paid.
But through His generosity, I can now forever celebrate,
And I can respond by being generous myself.
Just a little bit of the generosity He gave will certainly go a very long way.

<u>The Mockery of the Cross:</u>

Crushed and afflicted,
Beaten and mocked,
Our Saviour Jesus hung on the cross.
Who would have thought,
That dying on a tree would succeed?
Surely, the battle had been lost.
He saved others, but yet He can't save Himself.
He's meant to be the King of Israel,
But where's the victory, if their King is dead on a tree?
No wonder He was mocked.
However, that was only one part of the irony.
Although it appeared death had won,
Jesus has succumbed.
He had a plan all along,
And while it seems odd,
He was to be despised, rejected, and crucified,
In order that the plan may be fulfilled,
That He could save us as the prophets foretold many years before.
Because while it had seemed lost, it was not over yet.
You see, Jesus rose up from the grave.
He won the victory.
Death has been defeated; nothing stands a chance.
Like Jesus cried out, "It is finished," on that cross,
He defeated the death that once reigned over our heads.
He took on our shame,
He took on the price we ought to have paid,
Offering new life for nothing we had done.
How will you respond to this wonderful news Jesus did for us?

Where does it say if you do this or that, everything would be good?
There would be no suffering to endure.
Yet there's actually no guarantee,
Quite the opposite, in fact.
Nobody in the Bible lived a life free of suffering or injustice.
So why should we?

<u>Glorify the Lord:</u>

We live in a crazy world.
The purpose of life is often ignored.
What were we created for?
Not ourselves, but for the Lord.
Yet constantly, people seek other things.
Whatever they desire is what they need.
But that's not the case.
What we need is Christ.
He is the one who sets us free.
We can stop chasing other things.
He is the one who truly satisfies.
He is the one who makes us alive.
He is the one who provides for our needs.
He is the only one that we should seek.
He deserves our praises,
Our full respect.
And so, may we give it to Him,
Our attention, thoughts, our entire being.
He is the one who made us and gave us life,
So He is the one who only satisfies.
Our purpose in life is to glorify Him,
So let's not get caught up chasing other things.

Christian Sinning?

Would you consider yourself a Christian?
If so, please stop and think.
If we are saved from God alone,
Does that mean we can keep living for ourselves?
Paul says no, right? We died to sin; how can we live in it any
longer?
And he's right, but do you find yourself constantly sinning?
But it's so easy to do... oh, this isn't too bad, surely it won't matter,
will it?
However, it cost God everything.
He died for you and me.
And although He rose back to life,
He didn't do it so we can sin again.
Although even though we still may sin in this life,
Doesn't mean we should do it when we know it's not right.
So, Lord, instead of thinking sin means nothing,
Help me to see the severity it will bring.
It ended up costing me nothing, while it cost You everything.

<u>Precious Life:</u>

Our life is so precious.
Each and every one of us is a gift to behold.
The world may depress us,
Although that's not how life was meant to unfold.
We were created uniquely made,
The glory of God in us displayed,
Is how life was meant to be designed,
Rather than our lives that are now frayed.
You see, God loves us so much.
He sent Jesus to die in our place.
He wanted His loving touch,
To be the one who holds us in His embrace.
And so may we each not forget,
The loving King who paid our debt,
So we can live with God in His wonderful grace.

6
Resurrection Series

These poems were written at MYC (a Christian conference) based upon resurrection. Through the messages and conversations that occurred, these were the psalms that unfolded.

I hope you enjoy this "resurrection series." I do not have individual titles for these "psalms" as they form part of the series.

In this section, I express here the inevitability of death, the hope of resurrection through Christ and the promise of that eternal life.

Death is gloomy, dark, and grim,
It is horrible, cold, and dim.
However, we try to make sense,
By bringing light to the darkness,
Or we try to avoid it at all expense,
Try to take away the hardness,
Try to bring hope to the situation.
But despite all our determination,
It is pointless.
We will all face death one day, regardless.
No matter how hard we try,
No matter how hard we push,
We are all destined for the grave.
And although we think we are in control of life,
That day could come despite any warning signs.
We could be fine one day,
And the next day, minute, or second, we are gone.
No more breath filling our lungs,
Just a lifeless corpse.
Is that all what life is for?
Who can live and not taste death?
Who can overcome the power of the grave?
Is there any hope at all to escape?

Was this the way it was meant to be?
Or is there something greater beyond the horizon that we can't
see?
Yet, who can escape the power of the grave?
Is it true our only hope is if our bodies are resurrected.
Some people say God's breath is the only way this can happen.
But how I am not so certain.

If you are a follower of God, you may believe,
That where God is taking us,
Shapes how we live.
Yet, is resurrection even a real thing?
Is that our only hope to taste life after death?
Will it help us escape the power of the grave?
But who can do such a thing?

Again, the question remains:
Who can overcome the power of the grave?
Who can escape the chains of death and reign victorious?
It seems like resurrection is the only way.
Who can live and not face death?
But raising from the grave just seems ridiculous.
Surely, even if you did, you would just die again.
It certainly wouldn't be eternal, would it?
Well, my Saviour Jesus changes that.
Quite a while back, He was killed and buried in a tomb.
Three days later, He rose up from the dead.
And I'm not just making up facts;
There's strong historical evidence.
Although all seemed to have been lost,
And death seemed to win again,
Death could not hold Him.
He's still alive to this day,
And because of that, we can now be the same.
If we trust in Jesus,
We will also be resurrected one day.
How? Because He will lead the way.
And if that's the case, where God is taking us,
Shapes how we live today.

Who can raise the dead?
Who can raise people back to life again?
Only God can.
It took His mighty power,
It took His mighty strength.
He made the new life concrete,
So it cannot be taken away.
God raised Jesus up above all other power;
He raised Him up to be the conquering King of the whole universe.
And therefore, we are safely secure in Him.
Because our Saviour conquered sin and death,
We can reign with Him once again.

Can you hear the groans of today?
A world that groans, something is not right.
There's sickness, mourning, pain, and death.
Among other things, just look around in the world, and it's easy to
see.
I certainly groan and cry out, "Why?"
What about you? Do you groan?
Because if you don't, perhaps you should.
Since did you know it's alright to groan with pain?
It's alright to groan with the pain as our God is saddened, too.
The world we live in today is fallen; it has rejected God.
So we should want a new life, and we can have that in Christ.
I cannot wait for that day where we will have new resurrected
bodies like Him.
Won't that day be glorious?
Oh, I can't wait for that day where I will be completely renewed
and will declare praises to my risen King, looking right at His face.
The world will cry out no more and instead declare and praise His
name.

7
Poems for friends; helpful to all

These few poems were written for a few friends of mine. With their permission, I am sharing it here.
Although it is written for them, and some things are specific to them, there are aspects of the poem that I think may be helpful to each and every one of us.

Feel free to read and, if applicable, change their name to yours; I am sure they won't mind

My dear beloved friend Esther,

What a beautiful, Godly lady you are!

I pray that this psalm I wrote may help and comfort you as you
have comforted me in the past.

This poem's not to remind you about me, but rather our great,
glorious God—oh, where do we start?

Esther, whatever you are going through,

I encourage you to chat with the Lord.

Although I am certainly not He, I pray through this poem, you may
see these basic truths: that God's chatting to you and to me.

When you say, "I am in this endless cycle,
What's the point of this meaningless life?
I work, I help others, but what is this for,
When I can't tell them about our glorious Lord?"

But oh, Esther, you can, although sometimes not with words.

Through your love and desire for God, they notice something a bit
absurd,
Something that is different, a strange hope you have inside,
Something that keeps you going when others may have quietly
resigned.

And when you do feel that you want to quit,

Just remember that God has some work for us to do,
Which is not meaningless but rather has eternal value.

And when you say, "I am incompetent; I don't know what to do,"
Recognise that it's God's strength working in you.

When pain and sorrow come your way, which eventually they will,
Remember the hope we have in God.
Remember that although we may struggle for a little while, our
Saviour did it too.
Remember, although these things are painful, there's a greater
plan in store,
Making you and me more like our glorious Lord.

One day, there will be no more pain or sorrow, but whenever that
may be,
Please keep pushing through, not on your own,
But through the power of our mighty King.
He will help you overcome any battle—just wait and see.
Remember, He is ultimately in control over everything.

Hear now His whispers to you, Esther, giving you strength right
where you may be:

My dear beloved Esther,

You love to help people;
I can see it in your eyes.
I love to help people, too;
That's why I laid down My life.

But just know that it's okay sometimes,
To stop and think awhile.
Rest in Me, just relax for a little while.
Know that I am there for you when you are in despair.

111

Know that I am there for you in times of joy and when happiness
fills the air.
Know that I am there for you no matter what the season brings.
It's My love for you, My precious child,
That will help and see you through anything.

Because without My love flowing through you,
You will drown in all that you do.
However, know you can do it as I'm at work in you.
I am the one that will sustain you through.

The love you have for others, you really got from Me,
But remember without My love, the world would still and always
be in a giant gloomy heap.
However, because I laid down My life and then rose up from the
grave,
People can be free to believe and live for Me again.

Therefore, share the great, glorious news of who I am,
But just know the world is not ultimately rejecting you but rather
Me, which they've done for centuries.

So, my dear beloved Esther, keep living your life for Me.
I will help you through, and people around you will see My love
overflowing through you out of Me.
Medicine and others will fail, as it has within the past,
But know I will never fail you no matter what you've done.
No, I will never leave you, even when it seems hard.
Please just find your rest and joy in Me, My child.

So, Esther, now that you've read this, I just invite you to pray.
Pour out your heart to our God forevermore today.
He always loves and cares for you; He always loves to hear your
voice.
Go on now; what are you waiting for?

<u>Nicole:</u>

Wonderful, majestic friend,

Bubbly, joyful, not obedient,

Thanks for being there.

Thanks for trusting me.

Thanks for the laugh and the tears we've already shared.

I'm so glad God brought us together, my friend.

Here are the words you asked for;
They are from God's viewpoint.
Listen to what He has to say,
As though He is speaking, not me.

Nicole, don't you see?

You mean the world to Me.
In the valleys, high or low,
Look for Me in every situation daily,
For there you will find victory.
Call upon Me, and I am there;
I'll give you My listening ear.
Know that I am always near;
Even the words you can't explain,
Will come to Me nonetheless.

So don't be afraid to cast your cares on Me.
Yes, it might not be easy,
But it will be worth it in the end.

How do you seek Me? I hear your plea.
Well, My child, don't you see?
All you need to do is just lean on Me.
Serve Me wholeheartedly.
Turn from evil.
Pursue peace.
Live humbly, doing what's right,
Lifting your soul only to Me.
Don't lift your soul to other things.
Read My Word every day.
So you know what I have to say.
In Me, you will find true, everlasting hope.
Know I love you unconditionally,
Even if you don't do these things.

But trust Me when I say,
You won't regret living with Me day by day.

8
Reflective Poems

There are some psalms I wrote that do not seem to fit nicely in the categories above, and so here they are.

This section carries poems that were hard to write, taking a few days or longer. It is also difficult to strictly put them into a category.

<u>True Diagnosis:</u>

Yet diagnosed with another thing.
All these problems are killing me.
However, really, they are not; my biggest problem is actually sin—
Sin, my rejection of God.
Sin is the one that actually kills me,
Not just in this life, but through all of eternity.
I need a Saviour to rescue me,
Because I can't do it at all, no matter how hard I try.
I constantly fail at being sin-free.
How amazing, though, is it that God gave Himself?
He suffered in my place, taking the guilt, power, and shame of sin
away from me,
So I can stand in His presence absolutely free.
Although I still sin, it has no control over my body.
It can no longer defeat me.
But rather, Christ, who is living inside,
Works in and through my life,
So that I may proclaim His wondrous power and glory.
Thank You, Jesus, that I can stand before You,
Righteous and holy through what You've done for me.

<u>Dress Code:</u>

You say, "Come as we are,"
But then some people say we need to dress a certain way.
I partly understand why; I mean, You do deserve our respect.
And I guess our dress code could be a small element.
You do also say, "Don't make anyone else stumble."
So, if that's the case, then our dress code matters.
But is it really meant to be that way?
Is it really important that's how we behave?
Because really, wouldn't it work both ways?
Therefore, please give us wisdom to know what to do,
Because ultimately, we want people to know You.

<u>Saved For a Reason:</u>

I come to You with all these thoughts and questions.
Other times, I just wonder how.
I marvel at Your presence
And then look at mine.
I'm reminded of who I was
And look at who I now am.
I question how I came to be,
Even though I understand how,
I don't understand why.
Why would You save a sinner like me?
That's just the greatest mystery.
Now I have a choice to make:
How I'm going to live day by day.
I want to choose You; I do.
But I need You to work in me,
To remind me daily, every minute, every second.
Otherwise, I may—well, will—become complacent.
Help me to look towards Your presence, Lord,
With more wonder than I had before.
Please keep changing, shaping, and moulding me,
Not just so that I will be ready for the new creation,
But others will be, too,
Through the work You do through me.
I'm praying, Lord Jesus,
Of more glorious stories,
Where people once dead became alive again.
Won't that be a marvellous end?

Choices:

Lord, I'm stuck at a crossroad.
I don't know what to do.
There's neither a good nor bad path,
As both are great choices to choose.
However, that just makes it harder to decide.
So please give me the wisdom to make this decision,
And please help me overcome this "what if" condition.
Because ultimately, Lord, whatever path I choose,
I need You to be leading the way, which You will,
No matter the pathway I take.
But right now, I pray, please help me, Lord, with this decision I make.
I'm still asking for Your guidance today,
And I pray that no matter what, I will every day.

Prayer,
Is talking to You...
What an amazing thing I can do!
There is no greater gift I can get,
Than to have a personal relationship with my Lord.
Yet, I rarely remember what a privilege it is,
And often succumb to more lower earthly things.
However, this isn't how it should be,
And so I humbly fall to my knees.
I ask You to please forgive me,
And to give me more of a desire to go to You.
I want to praise You, thank You, just simply talk,
But remind me to also listen to Your voice.
In order to build a relationship, both sides need to give,
And because I know I often just take,
I ask that You please change my heart today.
But ultimately, I pray, may Your will be done always.
May this relationship not only remain but grow, stronger, deeper,
and more personal each day.

<u>God View?:</u>

What's the bottom line?
How do we view God?
Is He just our taskmaster, or perhaps a Servant to us?
Does God control our life, so if we make one mistake,
We would not survive another day?
How else would we respond,
If God was our taskmaster?
Everything we do comes with a cost.
We would need to be perfect.
To keep going on.
Yet if we view God as only our Servant,
We would not have a personal relationship,
As the only time, we would go to Him,
Was if we needed something from Him.
How crazy is that?
However, know we can never disappoint God,
Because we were never holding Him up, He was holding us.
He is holding us up with His righteous right hand.
What amazing news that brings for all who believe!
We don't need to be glorious because God already was.
We don't need to be majestic,
Because it's not about us.
God is majestic, glorious, and more greater than we ever thought.
He's our loving Father,
Greater than any earthly one.
He gives us security, protection, and love.
He desires to have a personal relationship,
And cares deeply about us.
Yet He's also a just judge.
Someday we will all give an account to God for what we have done.

But we do not need to be afraid,
Because while yes, God is just,
He took the punishment for us,
Through Jesus, His Son.
And so if we trust God as our Saviour,
One day, we will be victorious through His redeeming blood.
Because Jesus rose to life again, we can be sure that we will too.
Jesus is our rightful King.
So may we honour and glorify Him.
While although yes, we are in the world,
Scripture still proclaims,
That as God's children,
As the ones He has saved,
No longer of the world do we remain.
Our God is glorious, majestic, far worthy of praise.
He never was a tough taskmaster.
And although it's good to serve,
May our motives be checked.
May we be reminded that we cannot earn God's acceptance,
Because God will never love us more than what He does right now.
He wants more of our presence than our service; He does not want
us to drown.
He's not a motivational life coach either,
Just giving us advice,
Ensuring our goals are met based on what we feel is right.
And as soon as it is inconvenient, we tuck Him out of sight.
Since God knows everything, only He is truly in control.
How this would work, I do not know.
Yet constantly we try.
Maybe we only think of God as the one who gets us out of trouble.
It doesn't matter what we do, as God will set us free.
But He's only ever needed when trouble comes knocking at the
door.
At every other time, no contact is given or found.
As long as it doesn't affect us, He can do as He pleases.

But then maybe God is our Genie,
No personal relationship needs to be had,
But we will still get what benefits us.
However, God wants our priorities straight.
Our primary mission is to join Him,
To seek and save the lost.
The things of this world will pass away,
But God will always remain.
So what is your God view?
Will He be your meaning of life?
To deeply know God, seek and behold Him every day,
Knowing God is majestic, glorious, and worthy of all praise.

Christianity is about teamwork.
We need each other's support.
We weren't made to do this alone.
It cannot be done well if so.
Just take, for instance, telling people about God—it can be hard.
While you may find it easy, others may not.
We were made to help and encourage each other in this work together,
But we were also meant to do this in love.
Say things that bring life,
Setting about Christ in our hearts,
Knowing He is our Lord.
If we do this, all our fears will wash away,
And service to our Lord remains.
But this is not an easy task,
And so we need to be reminded through others' words and the word of God.
We need to be reminded that there's a greater faith and hope in the world to come.
We need to be reminded that Jesus is Lord of all, not our fears or ultimately us.
May we continue to help and encourage each other in love,
So on that final day, we will stand before God together as one.

Millions of people die each day without hearing Your word.
I'm grieved at this, struck to the heart.
But yet I cry out,
"What can I do, God?
Because now that I am dependent on medication,
One that is only affordable over here,
How can I tell Your gospel overseas?
Where more people are mostly unreached?
Well, yes, in Australia, there's still plenty of need.
At least they have the means,
To say yes to You, their King.
But what about those who don't?
How would they know unless people go?
Why can't I be one of them?
Please, Lord, strengthen me as I do not know."

<u>True Identity:</u>

Isn't it crazy to think we were already made in the image of God?
Created in His image,
Yet we threw that all away,
To chase a new life, looking for things to inform us who we are.
However, we already have an identity—one with God.
That's who we truly were.
So, I am trading back the life that once was mine.
I can now do this only through Christ,
Because of His saving grace.
I am once again restored and made in God's image,
Defined by Him and no other thing.
I went back to my Father,
Right where I should be with what Jesus did for me.

May we be a servant to God...
Give Him our everyday ordinary life—
Sleeping, eating, going to work, and whatever else we may do.
May we bring it all before God, our King,
As a humble offering.

<u>Contradictions in the Cross:</u>

The cross—
The cross of Christ changes everything.
It has many meanings and is a great contradiction:
A symbol of violence and death but also of peace and life.
The cruelest human punishment designed,
To bring the slowest and most painful death known to man.
But in Christ, it now gives life.
Seems impossible, right?
It's a symbol of hate but also of love.
We hated God so much we wanted to put Him to death,
And put us in His place instead.
But His love for us shone through more.
Instead of giving us what we rightly deserved, for rejecting the one true King and Creator,
He gave His life to restore and save us.
A symbol of the greatest love we could ever know.
And as the cross brings accusation and sin, forgiveness, and purity are found within.
It wasn't really Christ who deserved to die, but us for all eternity.
Yet He was accused wrongly so we could be restored, forgiven, and made right,
Again, with God the King through Christ.
Jesus cleared our debt so we could be set free.
And as you look into the cross, brokenness and wholeness comes along.
Christ was beaten so we could be made whole.
We don't need to hold onto our past, hurt, pain, or problems anymore.
Jesus has taken them away if only we let Him hold our brokenness.
Although all seemed to be lost,

Everything was gained.
Although destruction and defeat seemed to win,
Jesus rose again, restoring and bringing about victory in Him.
While yes, we may feel broken now,
We can be made new again.
Because of Christ on the cross, this is not the end.
Rather, despite the contradictions within the meaning of the cross,
Through Jesus and the new meaning it now brings,
Abundant life is found in Him.
Thank You, Jesus, for changing everything.
Now, simply to the cross of Christ, we cling.

<u>Hell or Not?:</u>

God is good.
He is the giver of all good things.
He made the world and all that is in it;
Therefore, good is in the world.
The good comes from Him.
But imagine a world without God—
No good would abound.
Good will cease to exist.
Wouldn't that be horrible?
It's hard to imagine a place without any good at all,
But unfortunately, it exists, commonly referred to as hell.
It's hard to talk about,
Hard to imagine such a place exists—
No joy, peace, love, or security.
Nothing.
Yet all these emotions bubble up inside of me.
I am angry and confused; I don't know what to do.
I am sad for the people who end up in that place,
And angry at God for letting it be that way.
But really, I have no right to be angry at God,
Just because my basic human mind can't comprehend all that is
going on.
Hell is a place we all deserve to be.
It's a place without God's loving rule,
Which we all turned from and rejected.
Yet I am confused—why did God save me?
While I should be rejoicing at the fact that He did,
I am burdened with the fact that others didn't give their life to
Him.
The real question I guess I am struggling with,

Is not why did anyone go to hell, as I believe that's where we
belong,
But why does anyone go to heaven at all?
Through Jesus, we now have a choice.
We can either choose the undeserved kingdom life,
Or what we already deserve—life without our Saviour Christ,
Life without Him and without any of His gifts.
That not only grieves me but God deeply.
And so He provided a way to save,
But yet still a choice has to be made,
To either accept or reject the gift He displays.
Why, I still do not know,
As I continue to wrestle with this myself.
All I know is that none of us deserve to go to heaven;
Rather, we belong to hell.
Hell exists.
It's truly awful.
So why aren't we warning people?
Why aren't we proclaiming more that because of Jesus' death and
resurrection,
It's something we no longer have to endure?
All I know is that if we truly love people,
I want them to forever enjoy life with God.
I want them to see and taste His just good love.
So why aren't I spreading the gospel to the world?

<u>Powerful Words:</u>

Words are powerful.
They can be used for great good but also can bring great pain.
Just think—once words are said,
You cannot take them back again.
Once they are out, they are out,
And the damage is done.
Even if you so desperately want to reverse the spoken words back
into your mouth,
You, unfortunately cannot.
Therefore, we need to be careful with the words we say,
To use them for great good instead of great pain.
I'm not saying don't talk; that's not at all what I mean.
But maybe just think before you say something you might later
regret.
Wouldn't it be cool if the words we used helped to build other
people up instead?
May our words glorify God,
Bringing praise and honour to His name,
Not dragging others down to build us up.

A little sparkle of joy,
Emerged from inside their mother's womb.
How precious to see, hold, feel, and touch this little one.
My adoration grew,
As I thought about this unique newborn,
And how they came to be,
At their parent's side so amazingly.
God had carefully knit this child together.
Each little piece He knew.
He loves and adores His new creation.
He cares about them further than the moon.
Despite the bumps along the way,
That would ultimately come knocking at the door,
The mysteries and discoveries for them to explore,
God still loves, cares, and has a great purpose for this little one.
It's amazing what He has done.
He's given us a marvellous gift—
A little bundle of treasure to hold and love.

We are all miracles.
Every single person in the world,
Is a living, breathing, walking miracle.
We were all created by God,
Not by chance but by design.
Yet there's still so much mystery about us,
That seems impossible.
Science cannot explain what is happening,
And sometimes, we begin to question why.
Yet, even so, we should never give up hope,
Because it's a miracle we are alive.
It's a miracle we are breathing right now.
Yet we know God turns the impossible,
Into living, breathing, walking miracles.

Christian education—
Christian education is not just a list of things to uphold;
It is about inward transformation shining out so bright,
That it cannot be folded up tight.
It far outshines any source of light,
As the light inside us is only Christ.

<u>No One Good:</u>

There is no one that is good,
Not even one.
We've all sinned and rejected God.
Yet so many people in the world today,
Say they are good.
They've lived a good life, keeping out of other people's way.
So, who are we to say,
They've sinned and fallen astray?
They didn't trust God in the first place,
And religion is what actually brings so much pain.
So how can we judge them,
When they have done good by staying away?
God is not their King, so they've done nothing wrong.
However, whether they like it or not,
God was the true Creator.
He is the rightful King.
And so, ultimately, they've rejected Him.
But let's, for a moment, put that aside,
And ask on the horizontal line:
Have you ever lied, cheated, or stolen?
Have you ever put someone down so that you could rise above?
Have you ever hurt someone intentionally, whether physically,
emotionally, or spiritually?
I think we know that not one human can say no honestly to all of
these things—
At least not truthfully.
And if you can, then it won't be long before you tick one of these.
So, in reality, I think it's clear to say,
There's no one that is good,
Not even one—
Well, at least not apart from God.

<u>What Does Love Even Mean?:</u>

Love—
It's a strange thing.
What does love really mean?

Tenderness, fondness, adoration,
Passion, affection, a deep devotion—
The act of caring and giving to someone else, yes, even more than
yourself.
Having someone's best interests and well-being as a priority,
Are only a few words to begin to describe.
Love has many senses, both as a verb and a noun.
It is difficult to explain what love is all about.
But one thing remains:
Love is commitment without condition.
To truly love is a selfless act.
It's not looking to get anything back.
Who can do that?
The greatest example of love ever bestowed,
Was given to us by God Himself.
He took Himself from the greatest throne,
Humbling Himself as a man on earth.
Perhaps you know this guy, Jesus,
Or perhaps you don't.
I'm going to tell you the story anyway,
So you can see and be amazed.
God had nothing to gain;
It was us that had run away,
From the beauty, glory, and significance God had created us with.
Even though we weren't deserving of this,
But what do humans decide to do?

Say no to the King and yes to what we want to do.
We went out into the world seeking someone else,
Whether that be an actual person or a material thing.
It doesn't matter as we strayed from our King,
And said no to Him.
But what did we gain?
Nothing but bruises, scars, broken bodies, and shame.
That glory that once shone had gone,
Too ashamed to run back to our Lord,
Or perhaps we still haven't stopped trying to find the perfect King
aside from God.
How foolish of us to think that we would be able to accomplish
this.
We hid, or perhaps are still hiding, not realising the power that
our King brings.
But what did He do for us?
He lowered Himself, became beaten and worn,
Not because He was powerless,
But because He was coming for us.
To rescue us so that we could go home,
Back where we belonged with God above.
So Jesus Himself became battered and bruised—
The love so deep He had within.
We didn't deserve this,
But loving us so unconditionally,
He calls us home to be with Him on His throne.
Will you accept this greatest gift of love,
That Jesus Himself gave to us?

About the Author

Amber Wise was originally from a small country town in Western Australia called Gnowangerup. She lived with her parents and 4 siblings. Having moved around in Western Australia for education and pursuing her career; she is now a teacher in the Northern Territory, moving there early in 2024. She became a Christian at a young age and has a heart and love for God, wanting to share that with others. Her favourite part about teaching in the private sector is getting to share God with her students. Amber also has many chronic medical conditions, which caused her to write some of these "psalms."

In this book, Amber presents a collection of 100 poems from the different seasons of her life. Each poem tells a tale about her journey and gives the reader insight into her heart. Her Christian faith, grounded in and guided by Christ, shines through her unique experiences. Every verse is a reflection of Amber's perspective, where she explores the laments, gratitude, wisdom, love, and power of faith. The poems resonate with her heart and universal human experiences.

She is currently working on a new book that will address some of this, looking at young adult experiences and how they have held fast to Christ despite pain!

www.ingramcontent.com/pod-product-compliance
Lightning Source LLC
Chambersburg PA
CBHW040830010826

48978CB00012BB/684